PATRICK and The **VIRUS** MONSTER

Patrick Lawson-Collins

Illustrations by Zara Lawson

This book is illustrated by Zara and written by Patrick.

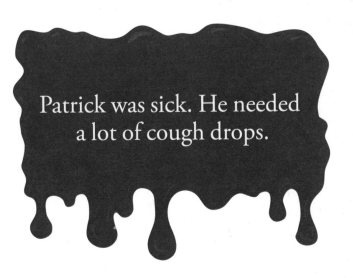

Patrick was sick. He needed
a lot of cough drops.

Patrick's parents are INVENTORS.

They decided to invent a machine to pull the sickness out of Patrick. It took several tries but they finally created a machine that would work.

Patrick's parents needed to test the machine. They had an old computer with a virus. The inventors put the computer on the virus machine and turned it on.

"It worked!" Patrick's parents said. The virus was gone.

Happy with the result of the test, Patrick's parents decided to try their invention on Patrick.

The machine worked!
The virus was pulled out of Patrick.

His parents were happy until they saw a small blob next to the machine. The blob grew and grew until it was the size of a refrigerator.

Then the blob did something even more amazing.
It opened a large red eye.

The virus monster blinked at Patrick.

Then it coughed, sneezed, coughed again, and busted out of the door, leaving slimy green mucus dripping down the broken door.

The slime monster moved pretty quickly for a big blob of snot.

Patrick quickly lost sight of the monster. He returned home, worried that his germs would infect others.

Patrick's mom turned on the TV and switched the channel to news.

The news anchor said that the slime monster was headed for Grant Elementary School.

Patrick shouted, "My school!"

He and his parents were so sad that they had unleashed the monster on the school.

They jumped into their van and sped to Grant.

Grant Elementary was **CHAOS!**

The virus monster arrived during an assembly. It oozed in and slid to the stage of the auditorium.

Suddenly, the monster started to grow bigger. It seemed to be breathing in air.

It got bigger and bigger until HA CHOO! The virus sneezed and covered the school with green goo.

Patrick and his parents watched as hundreds of students ran out of the auditorium covered in snot.

The kids were sneezing and couching. Patrick knew he must stop the virus. And he needed his parents' help.

Patrick's parents drove him home.

"Can you make a giant handkerchief out of the cough drops and cold medicine?" Patrick asked.

"Sure," said his mom. She pulled out a machine she had built to weave Giant Rhino diapers. She turned it on and threw the cough drops and medicine into the top.

Patrick grabbed the giant hanky and put it in his backpack.

They went back to the school to destroy the virus monster.

When they got there, the monster was holding Patrick's teacher and sneezing on her. "Gross," said Patrick.

"Hey, snot face," Patrick yelled. "Put my teacher down and come get me!"

The virus slowly dropped the teacher to the ground and oozed towards Patrick.

Patrick ran to the front of the school
where an old cannon sat.

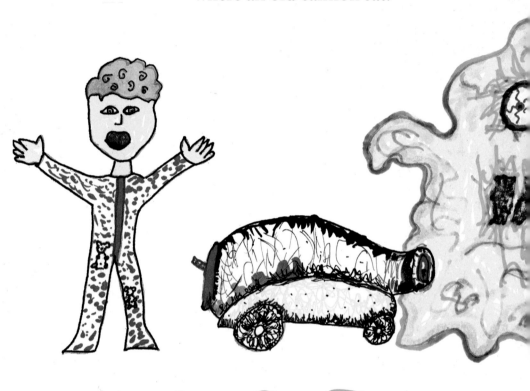

He called to the monster,
"Come over here, monster!"

The monster slid faster. Patrick jumped out of the way and the monster smacked into the cannon.

Patrick lit the cannon and shot the virus towards his mom, who had tied up the giant hanky.

The monster hit the hanky and became covered in the huge tissue.

The monster ran into the wall.

Patrick ran to the monster and punched the
tissue into the monster.

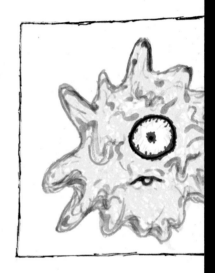

The monster dissolved out of existence.
The school was saved!

Patrick was no longer sick and everyone
was safe.

THE END.